T0113821

# The Other Girl

# The Other Girl

## Utpal Dasgupta

authorHOUSE®

*AuthorHouse™ UK*
*1663 Liberty Drive*
*Bloomington, IN 47403   USA*
*www.authorhouse.co.uk*
*Phone: 0800.197.4150*

*Published by AuthorHouse  04/08/2015*

*ISBN: 978-1-5049-4005-4 (sc)*
*ISBN: 978-1-5049-4008-5 (e)*

*Print information available on the last page.*

*Any people depicted in stock imagery provided by Thinkstock are models, and such images are being used for illustrative purposes only. Certain stock imagery © Thinkstock.*

*This book is printed on acid-free paper.*

# (1)

My name is Arijit Majumdar. I am a senior executive in a multinational bank. I started my career as an Upper Division Clerk in a government office at 22. However, within a few months I left that job and joined this bank as a junior officer. Since then, by dint of merit, and of course some luck, I have had timely promotions. At present, I am holding this senior executive position. It is a position of prestige, power, and status in society. I am 35 now.

In the course of my career, I have been pretty mobile, my employment being transferable in nature. I have served at various locations in India, and had a three-year stint abroad. I am posted at Calcutta for quite some time now, and may receive marching orders any day.

I married Shreya at the age of 24. She was 22 then. We have a son, Soumyajit, who is nine now. He studies in fourth grade in one of the best schools at Calcutta. I lost my mother when I was a child. I hardly remember her face. My father, too, died when I was quite young, and before I could finish my studies. I have a sister, eight years my elder, married to a state government officer. They have two children - a daughter and a son.

Shreya is the youngest of one brother and two sisters. Her parents are staying quite near our place. Her brother is in service. He is staying at New Delhi. He is married and has a daughter. Her sister stays at Bhopal. Her husband is a lecturer at a local college there. They have two sons.

My wife and I share some common passions. One such passion is Tagore. Our generation of Bengali intellectuals were split into two distinct groups - one was passionately opposed to Tagore and the other just the opposite. We did not belong to either group. In fact, we did never have any pretension or urge to project ourselves as intellectuals. We were simply infatuated with Tagore. This infatuation made our acquaintance possible.

I was doing my graduation during those days. I was the member of a very good reference library near our college since my first year. It was my final year then. I used to spend hours in the reading room of the library during off-periods and after college hours.

I was rather a shy chap and a loner. I did not have many friends. I was preoccupied with my studies and when I was not studying I used to read Wordsworth, Keats, Browning and other English poets, and certainly Tagore. I was quite happy in my self-contained environment.

But that year, at college, a girl started upsetting my environmental equilibrium. She was tall, slim, very fair, pretty, and with a pair of very lovely eyes. She seemed to me to be the most beautiful woman in the whole world. I felt very unhappy that I did not know her. I felt a strong urge to talk to her, to be her friend. But, alas! I could neither gather enough courage, nor invent any plausible excuse to talk to her.

I began to daydream that one day all of a sudden, there would be a violent student unrest at the college (it was very common at Calcutta during those days). The college authorities, sensing that the situation was beyond control, had called the police. There were bomb explosions, police firing, *lathi* charge, arrests, and absolute chaos all over the place. She was standing in a corner, bewildered, her terror-stricken eyes nervously looking for help.

I rushed to her side, and asked, "Where do you stay?" She gave a grateful look and stammered, "N-not very far away from here." "Come on," I said elegantly and escorted her back home. However, as ill luck would have it, there would be no student unrest at all. It left me as unhappy as ever.

One evening, I was studying at the library reading room. She came along with a friend and occupied the seats opposite mine. I felt a surge of happiness within me. It was the evening rush and there was not much choice, but it made me happy to imagine that she preferred the table as she had found me there. Rest of the evening, I pretended to study, but in reality, stole several glances at her. However, they were engaged in their studies, taking notes now and then. After about an hour, they left. I left immediately thereafter, with a broken heart.

After that evening, I found her at the library quite often. My longing for going to the library was greater than before. It gave me a sort of satisfaction of being with her, to enjoy the pleasure of her company from afar. I was unsuccessfully in pursuit of a chance to talk to her, but that possibly would never come. However, one day, I could manage a break!

It was my turn that day to find the reading room almost full and the seat opposite hers vacant. She and her friend were leafing through a volume of Tagore's works and talking to each other in a low voice. Instead of concentrating on my own studies, I tried to eavesdrop in their conversation. It seemed that they were trying to locate one of Tagore's poems in the volume but did not know the first line to search from the alphabetical index.

They were, in course of their exploration, repeating one or two lines from here and there. I immediately recognized the poem, though it was not one of Tagore's more popular pieces. I felt an uncontrollable urge to help them, but could not find my voice. Unhappily, I made futile attempts to take notes from my book. After about ten minutes, I had a feeling that they were preparing to leave. I could not believe my ears when I suddenly said, "Suppose I tell the first line of the poem..." and then felt embarrassed and stopped abruptly.

They both looked up, and she, with a smile implored, "Ple...e...e...z." I told her. They leafed through the alphabetical index and found it. "You like Tagore?" she asked with curiosity. "I *love* Tagore," I replied, "and you?" "I do too," she said.

She told that her name was Shreya and her friend was Tapasi. They were in their first year at college studying English literature. They were very fond of Tagore and trying to discover the influence of Wordsworth and Browning in Tagore's poems. I informed that I was a finalist in Commerce from the same college. Although I was not a student of literature, I enjoyed reading Tagore, Wordsworth, Keats, and Browning, and poetry in general. That evening, on my way back home, I was feeling as light as a swallow.

From that day, everything seemed so easy. We exchanged smiles at the college, went to library together. I did not have to devise any pretext to sit by her side or to steal a glance or two to enjoy her charm. We would exchange our feelings quoting lines from Tagore's poems. Tapasi was a great company too, but most often, she, with a naughty smile, would go away leaving us alone.

Everything was going on well. However, when my final examination was just two months' away, I lost my father. He suffered a massive cardiac arrest, and everything was over within forty-eight hours. My sister and her husband insisted that I went and stayed with them until I finished my studies and got a job, which I accepted after some initial hesitations.

My sister's invaluable support and Shreya's friendship gave me the requisite strength to tide over those hard days.

# (2)

My employment requires a lot of travelling. I like it. Besides official tours, we (Shreya, Soumya, and I) usually go out at least twice every year. During Soumya's summer vacations, we visit some hill stations or cooler places. And in winter, around Christmas, our favourite choice is a seaside. We look forward with eagerness to these time offs and have always enjoyed them. These escapes make us feel fresh and recharged.

But when I look back at my first experience in travelling, it gives me a mixed feeling. At that time, I just joined a government department as a clerk. I was still staying at my sister's place.

There were more people at the office than work. Therefore, my colleagues spent most of their time talking and gossiping. They had endless topics to discuss ranging from politics, to sports, to films, to travels and so on. I could not readily participate in their discussions for my experience was limited, but I was a fascinated listener. Stories of their outings and travels, for the most part, caught my imagination.

One day a colleague began a conversation claiming that Darjeeling was the best place to spend a holiday. He went there several times. He asserted that Darjeeling was the most beautiful of all hill towns. He told about the toy train to reach Darjeeling from NJP, about the *Kanchenjunga,* about the sunrise at Tiger Hill, about *Mirik,* and many more things about Darjeeling that were interesting.

Another member disagreed with him saying that *Puri* was a better holiday destination. With a nostalgic touch, he spoke of the lovely Puri beaches, its golden sands, and gentle sunshine, of the long, uninterrupted view of the horizon across the sea, of its colourful sunsets, of the *Jagannath* temple. In no time, the two were locked in a verbal duel while others enjoyed the battle from sidelines, throwing one or two comments, every so often, to keep the *mêlée* rolling.

It all seemed very incredible, very exciting. My father, a schoolteacher, was a very health conscious man. I travelled with him several times to *Madhupur* and *Giridih,* which were considered health-resorts. But Darjeeling and Puri seemed to be destinations of a different sort. My imagination ran wild and I felt that life would be futile if I did not set eyes on these places.

But Darjeeling? Or Puri? - a choice had to be made. I chose Darjeeling and revealed my plans to my sister. It was January - when winter was at its worst. My sister and brother-in-law felt that I was mad. Shreya and Tapasi too shared the same notion. But my resolve was firm and I was not to be dispirited so easily. So I booked a ticket, and one evening boarded an NJP (New Jalpaiguri) - bound train.

# (3)

This was my maiden night trip alone. I had some previous experiences of night journeys. But, by no means, all by myself.

I carried two suitcases full of warm clothing. Everyone at home petrified me about the damp and chilly weather of Darjeeling at that time of the year. "Take care of your belongings," my sister furthermore warned me, "you may lose them if you aren't watchful."

My brother-in-law escorted me to the Railway Station. He located the compartment that I was to travel in, and chained my suitcases below the berth allotted to me. The whole compartment was overflowing with people. They were talking loudly to each other, children crying, vendors making last minute efforts to sell - the compartment was quite clamorous. It was so overcrowded and noisy that I felt out of breath. My spirit dampened a little. However, as departure time of the train approached, the crowd thinned, and the raucous died down. At last, the train started moving. My brother-in-law waved at me and left. I suddenly felt very lonely, very helpless.

As the train gained speed, I sat down to study my co-passengers circumspectly. I got a lower berth. Besides me, there was a family of three -. a middle-aged couple and a daughter, and another young couple all by themselves. Two persons, perhaps friends, occupied the two side berths. They were continuously talking and laughing at each other.

The girl, whose name was Romi, was being frequently reprimanded by her mother, for holding out her hands out of the window. Her father was busy with a Railway timetable. The young couple – sat side by side – were talking softly between themselves.

I wondered if any one of them could run away with my suitcases! The possibility seemed very remote. Nevertheless, I could not dismiss the idea altogether and resolved to remain alert.

After a short while, everyone started preparing for sleep. I took out an air-pillow and a blanket from my suitcase, locked it securely, examined the lock of the chain, and then reclined on my birth covering myself with the blanket. Someone put the lights off. Only a blue night lamp remained glowing, creating an uncanny yet dreamy ambience.

Tranquility descended little by little in the compartment except for the murmur of human voices from afar, an occasional sob of a child and a grotesque harmony of snores of dissimilar blends. The train hurtled past through the darkness producing hackneyed sound of motion of wheels on the rail. In the midst of all these and the rhythmic swings of the moving carriages, I felt very sleepy and could not keep my eyes open any longer. When I woke up, the daylight was streaming through the windows. The train was still in motion. My fellow passengers were busy finishing morning chores. I, too, joined the rush. We reached NJP around quarter to eight. The first phase of the journey was over.

*\*\**

A porter took hold of my luggage and guided me to the narrow-gauge section of the railway station, where I boarded the Darjeeling-bound toy train. It had five or six blue-coloured miniature compartments with two baby engines – one attached at the front to pull the train – and the other at the rear end to push it forward. The porter managed a window seat for me.

The journey towards Darjeeling began a little after nine. The train lazily glided through the tea plantations providing panoramic views of the valley.

The compartment was mostly full of local people. The train stopped at several stations. I asked one old woman - who was sitting opposite me - when the train would reach Darjeeling. "In the evening," she replied uncertainly. My heart sank and a feeling of uneasiness rose within me. I cursed my friends who prevented me from booking a hotel room from Calcutta. "Don't worry," they assured, "it's off-season; finding a room won't be difficult." I wondered if that would be easy at an unknown place after sundown.

At half past two, we reached *Kurseong*. I was quite hungry and bought a lunch packet from a platform vendor. It was after the day's end that we reached *Ghoom*. I was told that it was the uppermost railway station in the world. However, in the darkness I could not feel anything extraordinary about it. "There!" exclaimed someone in the compartment, "the *Batasia* loop." But I could not make out anything.

I wore a woolen pullover over my shirt and kept some warm clothing handy in one suitcase in case I needed them. I did not experience any unusual chill till then and wondered why people frightened me about Darjeeling winter.

Darjeeling railway station was very badly lit.

It was almost as dark as Ghoom. Before I could get down, an old man - of Nepalese origin by appearance - came towards me and asked if I needed a hotel room. I hesitated a bit and then said, "Yes." "Give me your suitcases," he said, "and follow me." I did not have much choice. Nevertheless, I asked intuitively, "Which hotel?" "Hotel Broadway," he said. "And the room rent?" I enquired. "Eighty rupees per day," he replied, "but forty for you."

I felt far from comfortable from his munificence. The man was a stranger and the place unknown. I looked around.

Everything looked gloomy in the darkness. Then I decided to try my luck. "Let's find out," I told him apathetically, and showed my suitcases. He secured them in a lasso prepared from a broad piece of cloth and placed them on his back. He fixed the other end of the lasso on his forehead and signaled me to follow him.

A sudden gust of damp, cold wind greeted me as soon as I stepped out of the platform. I felt I was chilled to my bones! Yet another realization came after I toddled for a couple of minutes. The path was not even, as we found at other places. At times, we were climbing down and at others going up. At places, slopes were very steep. My companion was frequently admonishing me against the hazard of losing control.

"Look, yonder," my escort signaled towards small irregular splodges of lights, hither and thither, discernible faintly through the fog. "We'll be at the hotel in a moment," he stated positively. I looked up. The entire passage had left me jaded and thoroughly fatigued. I longed for a wash, some food and a bed to sleep.

The man was as good as his words. In a few minutes, we were climbing up the stairs of Hotel Broadway leading to the Reception. The room was comfortably warm. The old man put down the suitcases from his back. I addressed the man at the reception desk and told that I needed a single room with attached bath. The receptionist quickly glanced through a register and said, "Single rooms without attached baths are presently available," and then seeing uncertainty in my eyes added, "You may have a double-bed room with attached bath." "What's the rent?" I asked and gave a quick look at the old porter.

"The actual rent is one hundred and fifty. But I can give you at hundred per day."

"But he promised me a room at forty only," I said and looked at the old man, "and I don't need a double-bed room."

"That's for a single room without bath, Sir," the man at the reception desk replied. "But I suggest you take this room. You get an excellent view of the *Kanchenjunga* from the room. In addition, the rent includes all the four meals. Then seeing me still in doubt, added, "O.K., I'll make it at seventy five for you."

"They must have some bad intention," I thought, but my weariness forced me to give in. I paid the porter, filled in the registration form and followed a Nepalese boy called *Ram Bahadur* who carried my suitcases to a room on the first floor.

It was a small but a decently equipped room. There was a double bed by the draped window covered with spotlessly clean milky-white linen, a dressing table and a closet on one side and a couch and a small centre table on the other. The floor was carpeted.

"When would you like to have dinner, Sir?" Ram Bahadur asked after he put my suitcases inside the closet.

"About half an hour later," I said. "I like to have a bath first."

"There's supply of hot water in the bathroom. Have a wash, Sir, but please don't take a bath at this hour."

He went to the bathroom and switched the geyser on. After that, he promised to bring dinner at 8:30 and left.

There was a spotless white towel in the bathroom, but I decided to use my own. The bathroom was very clean and dry. All along, I had a nagging feeling that behind all this graciousness, these people had some ulterior motive. I was not sure if I were overly nervous. A few years later, when I went to Shimla (this time once more during winter!), with Shreya, after our marriage, I learnt that hill people were very simple and honest. During winter, hotels lure tourists by offering handsome discounts on food and lodging.

I decided not to have a bath. I drenched my towel in hot water and sponged myself thoroughly. And that was the most unpleasant error of judgment that I made at Darjeeling! It never got dehydrated during my three-day stay there. The worst part of it was that every time I squeezed it, it gave out plenty of water! So I had to use the hotel's towel after that.

Ram Bahadur brought dinner exactly at 8:30. It was more than one can have, with several courses ranging from plain rice, *chapattis, dal,* fries, vegetable curry, fish curry, mutton and sweet dishes. I was hungry and the aroma was very good, but it failed to enchant me. The same disquieting feeling troubled me. I told him to take away the mutton and the *chapattis* and some of the rice.

Ram Bahadur informed that there was a dining hall and I had a choice of having my meals there or at the room. He requested me to keep the utensils outside the room after I finished and wished me good night.

At Calcutta, I was accustomed to dress lightly at bedtime. Clad in a *kurta* and a *pajama*, I went to bed. Oh! It was a bed of ice! I covered myself with both the blankets and tried to feel warm. Nevertheless, the needed warmth would not come. So I took out my own blanket from the suitcase and covered myself with all the three one upon another. Then I tried to be asleep.

If I was asleep for long I did not know, but woke up abruptly to find that I was quivering in cold. My head was as heavy as lead, the ears and the nose were numb with chill and I could not feel my limbs at all! After a while, somehow, I managed to reach for the woolen dressing gown from my suitcase, wrapped it around me, put on a monkey cap and a pair of woolen socks and went under the blankets again. Now I felt more at ease and the rest of the night passed off peacefully.

A knock at the door woke me up. The room was overflowing with soft morning radiance. As I opened the door, a smiling Ram Bahadur wished me good morning. He brought morning tea for me. He went to the window and pushed the curtain aside. The room was filled with bright sunlight. And as I looked beyond the window, my heartbeat quickened. Unfurled before my eyes the prodigious *Himalayas,* which I had seen only in black-n-white photographs. The snow-clad peaks radiated orange gold colour of the early morning sun.

"It's the *Kanchenjunga,*" said Ram Bahadur pointing to a peak, his eyes shining. "Splendid!" I exclaimed.

After a hot bath, I felt very fresh. Breakfast was also served very promptly. I dressed comfortably and on a second thought donned the monkey cap too, and came out of the hotel. When he was serving my breakfast, Ram Bahadur was ardently telling me about the various conducted tours available for sightseeing. However, I did not make up my mind as I walked out of the hotel.

"Uncle!" I heard a call from behind. Then sound of running footsteps and a pull on my elbow. Romi; I recognized her instantly. "Oh! You're looking very funny!" she started giggling. "You feel so cold?" I smiled and took the monkey cap off and shoved it into my coat pocket.

"Don't be a bother." Her mother said as she reached us. She was breathless from the brisk walking along the irregular topography. "I'm enjoying Romi's company." I told her truthfully, with a smile.

Romi held onto my arm and said, "Uncle, we are going to the zoo. Please come with us." I felt a keen desire to do so, but hesitated. She looked at her mother and pleaded, "Ma, please tell uncle to come." Then seeing her father coming, she let go my hands and ran towards him saying, "Papa, Papa, tell uncle to come along ... *please.*" He smiled at his daughter and then at me. I smiled back and wished him good morning.

Despite initial wavering, I thankfully accepted their proposition. Without wasting much time, we embarked on a conducted local sightseeing tour. Although Romi's prime attraction was the zoo, we also went to the Himalayan Mountaineering Institute and Museum, Botanical Gardens, Happy Valley Tea Estate, the Tibetan Refugees Self-Help Centre and a few other places on the way. Post-lunch, after a short rest, we set off for *Kalimpong* - a three-hour ride - and saw the *Tharpa Choling* Monastery there. We were greatly exhausted at the end of the day but unbelievably thrilled all the same and made our plans for the next day.

# (4)

Some attendant of the tour operator waked me up around three in the morning. "Tiger Hill! At the Jeep Terminus by three twenty five. Leaving for Tiger Hill at three thirty sharp!" I heard him repeating the message at some other rooms too. Feeling lazy at first, but then got up and was ready within fifteen minutes. As I opened the door to go out I found a smiling Ram Bahadur ready with the morning tea. I felt very thankful. I was at the jeep terminus in time.

Some ten to 15 passengers including children had been waiting in the misty obscurity. Four or five jeeps were being warmed up. Romi and her parents turned up just in time. Romi seemed to be grim. Her mother smiled and said, "She's annoyed at having to leave bed so early."

Romi leaned against her mother's arm and slept all the way to our destination. When we reached, the sky had begun to brighten. We hurried to take a good position at the viewing gallery. Thick fog all around made our vision extremely restricted. As the brightness improved, it was revealed to our great disappointment that the sky was very cloudy. The sun, concealed behind the cloud, turned dull red, then crimson and finally golden yellow. Sunrise at Tiger Hill remained an unfulfilled dream.

On our way back, we had a short halt at the Ghoom Monastery. We reached hotel just in time for breakfast. Two hours later, we were on our way to Mirik. This time I found my sweet little friend in her spirits once more. She picked up a few friends of her age during the journey and on reaching the lake, flew around with them like a butterfly much to the dislike of her mother but with the unspoken encouragement from her father.

While returning in the evening, our vehicle made a brief stop-over at the Nepal border and we literally walked into a Nepalese town full of shops selling foreign goods. We did not make any purchases, but many did, only to be harassed by the Indian Customs at the entry/exit point.

The following day, we did some shopping and took several rounds along the Mall and around. The next day Romi and her parents left for Gangtok. Romi was sad at the time of parting. She insisted that I too accompany them, her parents also requested. But in spite of the excitement of the past three days, I was feeling terribly homesick and boarded a Siliguri bound bus to catch the evening train to Calcutta

Thus, my unaccompanied excursion ended. While I was happy to be back to my customary schedule, I felt a keen desire to make many such expeditions in future, but never solitary another time.

A few months later, I left for Delhi to embark on my present career. When our matrimony was finalized I asked Shreya about her preference for a seaside or a hill station trip after marriage. "To hill stations in summer and sea-sides during winter," she said, and added with a mischievous grin, "every year!"

# (5)

We planned a trip to Bhopal this summer. Shreya's sister and brother-in-law had been inviting us since long. Soumya and Shreya sat down together to meticulously develop our schedule. It was decided that we would make a stop-over at Delhi for a couple of days. Shreya's brother and his family would also come down with us to Bhopal.

While my son and wife were busy working out our itinerary, arranging for tickets, etc., I was engaged in processing a proposal for financing a large tea garden in Assam. It was a large project, and if accepted, the financial stake of our bank would be quite substantial. Several technical aspects required thorough examination. A host of legal formalities needed compliance. A visit to the garden was also necessary.

I would be away on holiday for about three weeks. Therefore, Mr. Dewan, my immediate superior, desired that I completed all paperwork and prepared my report before I left. I remained busy conferencing with the Company directors, lawyers, and our legal and technical experts about various aspects of the proposed finance. I was returning home very late every day. Soumya and Shreya would eagerly wait to bring me up to date with the developments.

Almost everything moved as planned. However visiting the location presented a minor problem. The garden was in Assam. It was arranged that Mr. Dewan and I would fly to Guwahati in Assam. From there, the Company car would take us to the garden – a 3 to 4 hour journey through the picturesque hilly tract. Mr. Dewan would take his wife and daughter with him. In view of our ensuing Bhopal trip, I decided to travel alone.

One or two days before the journey, some insurgent groups active in the area, struck on several vehicles plying through that road and massacred a number of innocent passengers. As a precautionary measure, the government closed the road for public use for the time being. The other route for reaching the garden was through Tripura, but a little indirect. I felt a bit worried as I was racing against time. "I'll take care of this," Mr. Dewan assured, "go ahead and enjoy holiday.".

Two days' before my journey date, I sat down with Mr. Dewan to discuss the project. I apprised him of the findings. He examined my report, sought clarifications on several points and seemed to be satisfied with it. After a short lunch-break, we resumed work. But I found Mr. Dewan a little restless this time. In spite of a comfortable level of air-conditioning, I saw beads of sweat on his forehead. He tried to give attention for some time. But his restlessness increased. "Majumdar, I'm feeling a little unwell", he said at length, "we'll finish it tomorrow." He left for home looking noticeably off-colour. Later on, I gave a call at his home. He had suffered a massive heart-attack and was taken to a nursing home.

The next day, our VP summoned me in his chamber. After a short exchange of pleasantries, he came directly to point. "I'm afraid Mr. Majumdar," he began, "you may have to defer your holidays a little. I would be grateful, if you could conclude the project before leaving. In a week or ten days it'll be over, I hope."

I was aware what was coming but did not give any hint to Shreya last night. Coming back to my chamber, I called her at home and told all about it. We were both worried about Soumya's disappointment. Moreover, the entire schedule would be upset – ours, as well as our relatives'. Therefore, after a prolonged talk, we decided that Shreya and Soumya would go as scheduled. I would join them later after I was through with the assignment. The next day I saw them off at the airport. All three of us felt unhappy at the time of parting. The sky was cloudy and the day wore a gloomy look. I headed for office from the airport.

# (6)

I was absorbed in my work throughout the day. The project was taking a considerable amount of my time. Several less important jobs remained unattended. I utilized the occasion to clear them out one by one. When I was free, I looked at my watch. It was almost eight in the evening. Although I was not in a hurry to return home, I was unaware of the extent of lateness. I started to pack-up.

There had been a heavy downpour, perhaps in the afternoon. The roads were waterlogged and the traffic in disarray. I slowly moved my car through the bottleneck, but there was disorder all over. The public transport system was totally disrupted.

It took nearly fifty minutes to reach Southern Avenue. All the vehicles were moving at snail's pace. At the turning, I suddenly noticed a girl waving her hand to attract my attention. She was clad in a synthetic blue *sari* – completely drenched – a lock of wet hair pasted on her forehead. I cast an inquiring glance.

She came near the car in hurried steps and asked, "By any chance, would Selimpur be on your way? I couldn't find anything for the last about an hour." I opened the door silently and signaled her to come in.

For the next three or four minutes we travelled silently except she mumbled her thanks as she came in.

It's not in my nature to strike an instant friendship. While I can adapt to any situation, I usually keep my reserve until and unless I feel a natural affinity towards a person. In fact, as she hesitantly settled down with her wet clothes, I felt worried about my car's upholstery, at least for a split second. But my mind was preoccupied with a more distressed feeling of having to return to a lonely home. I tried to start a conversation to get rid of the feeling.

"Visiting a relative?" I asked.

"I teach a small boy here." She replied.

We again fell silent for sometime. But the conversation lightened my heart a little. I thought to myself that the she might be studying in a college and earning her pocket money from private tuition in the evening.

"Come here every evening?"

"Except on Sundays."

I started feeling grateful that it rained that evening and I chanced upon someone to divert my mind. Suddenly, I felt an unusual kinship with the girl.

In front of a small lane, she asked me to stop. She would get down. I asked her name. "Arati," she replied, "Arati Halder." "Be there tomorrow," I told her, as she got down, "it happens to be my way back home every evening, except on Sundays." She smiled her thanks and disappeared into the alley.

The maid had kept the dinner ready on the table. I was famished; so did not waste any time and sat down to eat. A lonesome dinner. I was expecting a call from Shreya. I lit one cigarette and leafed through a magazine. Subconsciously, however, I thought if that girl would turn up the next evening.

The telephone rang. Soumya was on the line, "Papa, we went to Mehrauli this afternoon – to see the Qutb Minar." He sounded excited. During the last one month, he had avidly read a number of travel magazines and books, and acquired almost an expertise in the history and geography of the places in his travel plan. He would have carried on, but his mother intruded. "when did you come back," her voice came. "Around half past nine," I said, "there'd been a heavy shower here." She then inquired if I had had dinner and gave one or two household instructions. "Are you missing me?" she queried. I said I did, which was quite true. "Please let me know when you are joining us," she said before saying good night with a note of melancholy in her voice. I began to feel very lonely and unhappy.

I had a disturbed sleep that night. Shreya was missing me. Soumya was also missing me but in a different way. Every night, he would tell me in detail about the events that took place throughout the day, share his joys and sorrows, and even secrets before going to bed. However, he had a companion – almost his age – in his cousin there. He would be busy with her.

The tea garden project could be finalized only after a trip to the spot. It all depended on how soon the road from Guwahati was reopened. The whole thing was uncertain. I would have to spend the mornings and the evenings alone. There was an unusual freshness about that girl. She was with me hardly for fifteen or twenty minutes. If she turned up tomorrow, I could spend some time with her, certainly, if she wished.

I woke up late next morning with a heavy head. Nevertheless, I quickly got ready, had breakfast, and left for office. It was a usual day. There was a call from the local office of the garden that the road might be reopened within a week. Throughout the day, I eagerly waited for the evening. At last, when it was seven, I left office. In my reckoning, eight would be too late. Yesterday was rather odd. I reached Southern Avenue within half an hour. She was not there. I was dismayed, but chose to hang on a little. Parking the car on the roadside, I purchased a pack of cigarettes and lit one. My endurance was rewarded.

After a while, I saw her, a big packet in a gift wrap in her hand. She looked at me and smiled.

"I thought you wouldn't come," I began.

"Honestly, I didn't take it seriously last night," she smiled, "thanks all the same."

"How about sitting somewhere for a while and chat over a cup of tea or cold drink?" I asked. There was a momentary hesitation in her eyes, but said right away, "OK, let's..."

We entered a local snack bar and ordered two Cokes. For a while, we sipped silently. I began to feel bad about obliging her to come. She was too polite to decline. Suddenly she said, "Do you smoke too much?"

"Four or five a day," I replied, "not much I suppose."

"No one ever smokes in our family."

"Staying with your parents?" I asked.

"At my sisters'," her face saddened a little, "I lost my father about a year back. My mother stays in Guwahati"

"Studying?"

"No, a school teacher."

We plunged into silence again. As soon as our drink was finished, she got up, thanked for the treat, and said, "Let's go. It's my daughter's birthday. She must be waiting …."

"You … married!" there was a trace of shock in my voice.

After a brief but uncomfortable quiet, she said stiffly, "My husband left me shortly after my daughter was born."

In the car, she enquired about my family. I told her that I was on a deferred holiday due to an office exigency. I was alone now, as Shreya, Soumya had already left for the trip, and I would be joining them, in all probability, within a week. I also thanked her for her company that evening as I loathed staying alone.

When we almost reached her place, impulsively, I took her hands in mine and said, "I'm sorry." She did not take her hands away but did not say anything either.

She got down at the same spot. I asked if we could dine together at some restaurant the next evening. Without saying a thing, she disappeared into the darkness.

# (7)

It was almost eventless, at the office, the following day. There was no news from Guwahati. Shreya telephoned to inquire about the progress. I was feeling a little restive and out of focus. Suddenly, I found myself engaged in a brown study, reliving last evening – uncertainly waiting by the wayside for Arati, the Coke break, my bewilderment, her calm revelation, my holding of her hands, her silent rebuff. I felt the embarrassment all over again. I chastised myself and tried to think about my wife, my son. I tried to feel how I missed them. True, I missed them very much. But I was shocked to find out that I was also missing that girl, whom I met only twice. It could not be love. Or was it infatuation? But why? Was it because I was feeling lonely in the absence of Shreya and Soumya? Was it frustration as my summer holidays were drifting away? Or longing for companionship?

I silently fought with myself and resolved to think about everything except Arati. I also resolved to visit

Mr. Dewan at Nursing Home. He was now out of danger and had been transferred to a cabin from ICCU. I tried to overlook the distressed emotion of missing a possibility of meeting Arati on my usual way back home. But I was firm in my determination.

I left office around 3-30 in the afternoon and headed for the nursing home. I was a little early and could not locate Mrs. Dewan or her son. I inquired about Mr. Dewan's cabin from the reception. Having nothing to do, I leisurely walked on the lawn and waited for Dewan's folks to turn up.

About ten minutes later, I saw Mr. Dewan's car entering the driveway. It slowed down and then stopped at the entrance and Mrs. Dewan got down followed by her son Ankit, who was of the same age as Soumya. But there was a third occupant who got down after Ankit. And to my utter surprise and with a sensation of relieved happiness I saw it was Arati! She smiled at me.

"Seems you know Arati", said Mrs. Dewan as she noticed my bewilderment. I was still recovering from the shock and could not answer, but Arati did. "He kindly dropped me home that day. It was so chaotic and I was stranded." She did not tell her about the next day, to my great relief. "Arati is like one of our family. She teaches Anku at school and also at home. He's also very fond of her. So is Mr. Dewan."

Like my son Soumya, Ankit was also studying in one of the best schools at Calcutta. I never imagined her to be teaching there! She was so simple in her appearance!

Mrs. Dewan had two visitor's passes with her. She told Ankit to take me to Mr. Dewan's cabin, while Arati and she would wait downstairs and go later. She said it would cheer Mr. Dewan up if he saw his friend. I protested. "He would rather be eager to meet his wife and son first."

After some shilly-shallying she gave in and went along with her son to Mr. Dewan. Arati and I sat down on a sofa in the visitors' waiting hall. It was an awkward silence between us.

As if understanding my predicament she spoke, "The Tea Estate Mr. Dewan and you are working on – my dad served as a doctor there – for 30 years." I was amazed. "You know about our project!"

"It was my place of birth. Spent there as a small child and grew up…." She sounded nostalgic, her eyes dreamy. A surge of emotion suddenly swept over me. I felt a strong urge to relive my early days, when life was so carefree, so easy.

She sensed that my feeling was in harmony with her own and said softly, "How I wish I could travel back in time and make the most of those wonderful days!"

We fell silent again. But now silence seemed to be more eloquent than a thousand words.

Mrs. Dewan came back. We looked inquiringly at her. "Very feeble … but the doctor said he was out of danger." She handed over the passes. "Please tell Anku to come down."

A frail looking Mr. Dewan was lying on a bed, eyes closed. Drip bottles were hanging from hooks attached to the bed and an array of tubes from the bottles came down and were attached to his hands. His son was sitting on a chair by the bed, his right hand placed on his father's arm.

As we moved near his head, Mr. Dewan opened his eyes and smiled faintly. Arati gently ran her fingers through his hair. Her look was sad but affectionate. She gave Anku her mother's message. Anku bade good bye to his father and nodded at us and left.

"Arati's a very good girl and know what Majumdar, she spent her childhood in that garden." Dewan was out of breath.

When the visiting hour was over and we were about to go, I offered to drop Arati at her place and she agreed.

# (8)

The road from Guwahati which was closed by the Government, was reopened. A news channel on television reported. The insurgent groups have agreed for a talk with the Government and declared truce. The news brightened me up. I thought of calling Shreya to give her the news when the telephone rang. Shreya had also learnt about it from TV and rang me before I could. She sounded relieved and happy.

"How long would it take to join us?" She asked. I made some mental calculations. "Six days – at the earliest." I said. She sounded distressed.

Next day I asked my travel agent to book a flight to Guwahati and rang up the tea garden people to arrange for transportation from Guwahati. Shreya had caringly kept my travel bag in readiness for the journey before she left. I dumped the official papers in it and left for airport. I would spend the night at Guwahati and set off for the garden early next morning.

I telephoned Mrs. Dewan from airport to enquire about the health of my colleague. He was fine and improving, she told. I requested her to tell Mr. Dewan about my Guwahati visit. She said she would and added that Arati was also taking the same flight to Guwahati with her daughter to see her mother. It was a day full of activity and it kept my mind away from anything else. The news did not upset my self-possession.

I found her waiting in the lounge for the flight. Her three-year old daughter was prancing around to the utter disapproval of her mother. As I approached and greeted her, her frown vanished. "A very pleasant surprise!" She smiled at me. Her daughter came running and jumped onto her mother's lap and said, "My mama!" "No mine." I teased her and sat by her mother's side. She put her two small arms around her mother's neck to secure her claim. "No! Mama – my mama – please tell him." Arati affectionately held her daughter closer and kissed her. "Uncle won't take your mama away!" She comforted her. In a few moments, she became easy and friendly with me.

When we reached Guwahati, it was almost dark. A person was waiting outside the airport to receive me. He was showing a banner with my name printed on it. Arati seemed to know him. I enquired if he could drop them at their place on my way to hotel. But she insisted that I spent the night at their place instead of staying in a hotel. Apu – her daughter – too, would not let me go. Reluctantly I agreed.

# (9)

The mother was as simple as the daughter. She was sitting outside on the lawn waiting for her daughter, when we arrived. She greeted me with a warm smile, before Arati could introduce the stranger to her. She was excited when told that I was on a visit to the garden where she spent the prime of her life with her husband and daughter.

I spent a very pleasant evening with the family. Arati's mother mused over her days at the plantation. About her husband – about how the plantation workers revered him – about Arati's schooldays – about her loneliness when her daughter stayed at Guwahati for higher studies.

Her tie with the garden, I felt, was unbroken.

"Never felt like visiting your old place – re-uniting with friends?" I asked her.

"I do; yes – and very passionately – at times. But …."

"But?"

"At others – I feel discouraged – not many old faces…"

"Would you – I mean the three of you - you may come with me – spend the day meeting friends…"

"You'll be needlessly troubled…"

"It'll be a pleasure – honestly."

She pondered over my proposition for some time and then looked at her daughter.

Arati spoke excitedly, "Why Ma! Mr. Majumdar will be busy with his work. We won't disturb him. Apu would see her Mama's place. And how happy would Mitra Auntie be!"

It was still dark, when we started next morning. And moist and foggy. During the first part of the trip, Apu remained asleep in her grandma's lap. But when she woke up, she talked like a chatterbox.

In about three and a half hours we reached our destination.

# (10)

It was late in the evening, when I finished my work. I could complete it in a more relaxed manner, in one or two days, but my impatience to join Shreya and Soumya at the earliest inspired me to take the plunge. I was satisfied but felt quite drained at the end of the day.

When I returned to the Guest House, Apu was fast asleep after dinner. Arati and her mother were waiting for me. They also appeared to be exhausted after day-long activity. However, their faces showed signs of fulfillment after reunion with their old friends.

After dinner, I lit a cigarette and sat quietly on a sofa in the verandah. It was drizzling. Everything was quiet and dark. I called Shreya before I left the tea garden office. She was happy to know that I would be joining them in two or three days.

Quietude too has a sound of its own. When we are in a known surrounding, we are so used to these sounds, we are quite oblivious of them. While I enjoyed my cigarette, I became aware of a mixture of different kinds of sounds. There was sound of cricket, hissing sound of wind, rasping sound of wet leaves, humming sound, sudden cracking sound and so on. I became quite absorbed for quite a long time, even after I had finished smoking. Now and then, thoughts of Shreya and Soumya would come up. When I called Shreya, Soumya was not there. He ought to be asleep by now. But his mother no doubt had told him about it. He must be very excited.

Someone nearby was humming a Tagore tune very softly. I was dreamily enjoying the sweet melody without making any effort to locate the singer. Shreya too would often hum Tagore tunes while doing her daily chores to my utter delight.

As I slowly came out of my reverie, I found Arati settled on a side of the sofa and humming. She was not in her usual Sari, but in a red nightdress and a woolen stole wrapped around her. I smiled at her. She too smiled back, but stopped humming.

"I was enjoying the tune." I said, a little disappointed.

"My father sang Tagore songs very well."

"Your Ma…"

"Retired. She enjoyed meeting her old friends. At the end of the day, she was exhausted. But she badly needed this break. Thanks."

"Oh! Not at all! Rather, I am supposed to be thankful. You saved me from spending the evening alone."

"Missing your son?"

"Yes… and missing Shreya too."

We remained quiet for some time. Then with a sudden surge of feeling, I took her hand in mine and asked with emotion, "Don't you miss your husband?"

She did not take her hand away, but said without any trace of emotion, "Why should I? He went away on his own."

"But, you have suffered.."

She did not let me finish, but shot back, "I was pained, when he left. Pain is inevitable, but suffering is optional. My father taught me to live in the present."

I could not help but silently admire the mental vigor of this simple girl. She made an impression, when I first met her on that rainy day. Every time, I met her after that, my respect for her became greater than before. But my masculine ego had always felt an inevitable desire to protect her!

Her hand was still in mine. I was enjoying its softness and warmth. She, as if, forgot that it was in my custody. Intuitively, I drew her close to mine and wrapped one of my arms around her and held her close to me as I would often do to Shreya. She did not stir or protest, but sat silently. I felt the pounding of her heart, the fragrance of her hair and softness of her body. How long we sat like that I do not know. My slumber was broken by Arati. "It's quite late, Mr. Majumdar," she said softly.

I held her tightly in my arms and kissed her several times on her lips. "Oh, no ... no...", she now protested. Without paying any attention to her protests, I lifted her in my arms and like a possessed person carried her to the bedroom. I laid her on the bed and settled beside her, caressing her breasts and other parts of her body. She made constant protests, trying frantically to free herself from my embrace.

I reached for the switch and put off the light. A dim blue night lamp kept glowing. I undid the knot on her nightdress and undressed her. Then I plunged my face on her breasts and kissed violently. Arati started sobbing. "Please …. Please …. Mr. Majumdar …. Oh no …. Please let me go…." Her body convulsively bent backward and forward and tried to resist my pressure.

But with the strength of a possessed man, I squeezed her with one hand and undressed myself with the other. Suddenly she accepted defeat and stopped all her resistance. Only her sobs were audible. I felt the urgency in me and raised her thighs and made my way deep into her moist and warm womb.

As my body moved up and down rhythmically on hers, I kissed her lips and neck and kept saying softly "I love you Arati!" The words were coming spontaneously and at that point of time, there was no other feeling in me except a very deep feeling of love for this simple girl.

All of a sudden she became convulsive again. She moaned and her body jerked and trembled and she put her arms around me and held me tightly. In a few moments, my whole consciousness was filled with an intense feeling of ecstasy.

I did not let her go away from my hold. She did not resist also. I must have fallen asleep immediately. In my sleep I felt that she gently freed herself from my arms, gathered her clothes, opened and closed the bathroom door. There was sound of flow of water in the bathroom. After a while, she gently opened the bedroom door and left.

Next morning, I did not get any chance to apologize to her for my brutish behavior. During our return journey, she remained reticent and not once her eyes fell on mine. Her mother too presumed that something was amiss and except for responding to the chirpings of Apu kept quiet.

The car dropped me at the airport and took the family home.

# (11)

As promised, I joined Shreya and Soumya at Bhopal in time. Both of them and others rejoiced seeing me. I also kept the tempo, but back somewhere in my mind, a nagging sense of guilt towards Shreya and towards Arati was hurting me.

I was in a dilemma, if I would come clean with the whole incident to Shreya. Being my wife she has a right to know the truth. But that would spoil their tour, which had already been damaged by my late appearance. So I postponed my 'coming clean' business till we reached Calcutta.

But I could not make up my mind to tell Shreya about Arati even after coming back. Somebody said, "You need not tell all the truth unless to those who have a right to know it all. But let all you tell be the truth." I did not remember who said it, but felt that Shreya had a right to know the whole truth. At times, I felt like telling her in a modified manner. But I felt it was unethical.

Subconsciously, I started a war with my conscience. Why did I want to tell Shreya? Was I feeling guilty to do a favor to Shreya? To clear my conscience? To be liberated from the nagging feeling of guilt for my improper conduct? But how Shreya would feel? Would she forgive me? Even if she forgave, would she not be pained by my infidelity?

My introspection started from another front. Very eager to confess my sin to Shreya? Why? Her presence in my daily life was making me uneasy? What about Arati? And the mental trauma she was suffering? Not putting me at unease as she was not there to make my conscience prick! Did I ever thought of apologizing? When I knew quite well where to find her!

I remained undecided about confessing to Shreya. But I thought I could at least in some way atone for my sin by apologizing to Arati. So every evening, Monday through Saturday, I waited in my car at that fateful crossing at Southern Avenue to find her. But alas! She would not be seen. I thought she might have changed her route. She used to go to Dewan's house to teach his son. But I did not dare ask Dewan. If Dewan knew of the incident – for the girl was very close to his family – he never gave any hint. But I decided against asking him.

Then I remembered that Arati was a teacher at Anku's school. I discreetly gathered information about school timings, which was not too difficult, as it was one of the best schools in Calcutta. I would take my car to the school during its closure time and wait on the wayside to get a glimpse of Arati and to talk to her, but in vain! I thought it to be too risky to ask the school authorities about Arati which might embarrass her.

Arati said suffering was optional. But the mental agony I suffered during the last six months was unbearable for me and I could find no way to opt out of it. Then, one day, I decided to ask Mr. Dewan.

"How is Arati? Still teaching your son?"

Mr. Dewan remained thoughtfully silent with eyes closed for a while. Then with great affection and with remorse replied, "That crazy girl! Left Calcutta about six month's back. Got some school job – I think at Dehra Doon. My wife implored her so … not to go. But, obstinate as she was …….. wouldn't listen to anybody. She was like one of our family."

"She writes, I hope?"

"Strangely, no. We've lost all contacts with her."

The news left me very distressed. During the last six months, I discovered to my great embarrassment that I was in love with Arati. My resolve to find Arati grew stronger.

I made discreet enquiries about Arati in and around all schools in Dehra Doon and once visited there too. But Arati was forever lost from my life!

# (12)

## Epilogue

After I made several unsuccessful attempts to find Arati, and when I faltered to make a clean breast of the affair to Shreya, I decided to write everything down truthfully in a diary. It was an endeavor to confess of my own guilt to me. This was about nineteen years back.

So many things have changed in our life during these nineteen years. I was transferred on promotion to New Delhi. I welcomed it as I longed to be away from Calcutta. Our Calcutta flat remained locked except for our occasional visits to meet our relatives. We purchased another flat at Delhi. Then I spent another four-year stint abroad. Shreya decided to stay back in Delhi so that Soumya's studies were not interrupted.

About two years back, I left the bank and started my own consultancy service based in Delhi. However, I was required to travel to other places in connection with my work. Soumya had gone to the States to study Economics at University of Illinois. After completing his doctorate he joined there as an associate professor.

Time has greatly paled those unhappy memories; but at times it comes back and torments me for a few days. However, a subliminal longing to meet Arati again, at least for once, have not died down yet. Shreya has remained a loving wife, a caring mother and a wonderful homemaker all these years without ever being aware of her husband's once in a lifetime infidelity.

I came to Allahabad on a professional assignment. Shreya went to Calcutta to visit her mother. I planned to join her there and spend some time with our relatives, specially with my elder sister and brother-in-law. As I reached Allahabad Railway Station around 9 p.m., I heard an announcement saying that my train to Howrah was delayed by six hours.

I made up my mind for a night long wait. I deposited my suitcase to the cloakroom, but carried the small handbag containing toiletry to the first class waiting room. It was also almost filled. But I managed an easy chair with hand rests and settled down there.

I had a disturbed sleep. There were frequent announcements of late running of several trains. The waiting room was full of people and their luggage. Passengers, finding no alternatives, made arrangements for their night spend on the floor. According to the latest announcement, my train would not come before 7 a.m. Some major accident near Kanpur was causing this delay.

In my dream I saw Soumya was standing near me and softly stroking my hand with his fingers. I woke up and saw a youngster of 17 or 18 years was saying to me, "Uncle, Ma… yonder … wants to talk to you."

I followed his gaze and for a few seconds my heart beat stopped. Arati! There she was, silently smiling at me! Except that she had put on some weight and was wearing a pair of glasses with black frame, which had somewhat given some solemnity in her persona, the minimalism in her looks was still there. She was dressed in a light blue cotton sari.

Suddenly a plethora of feelings and emotions rose in me! How madly I tried to find her out – to meet her just for once – to apologize for my foolish conduct – to share some of her woes! Somehow, I managed to fight back my tears. I got up from my chair.

"This is my son, Shubhojit", said Arati. "Shubho, touch uncle's feet."

I took Shubho in my arms. I ran my fingers affectionately through his hair.

"Which class you're studying in?"

"Got admission at IIT, Kanpur." He replied.

Arati glanced proudly at her son.

"Staying at Allahabad?"

"No, Delhi …"

"Delhi?" I turned to Arati with incredulity.

"I work in a Government school in Delhi. Came to Kanpur for Shubho's admission."

"How is Apu?"

"Doing her PhD from Allahabad University."

"So it was not … Dehra Doon …? I heard you …"

"Been there for a few months. Then this offer came."

"We moved to Delhi almost at the same time." And then remembering something, I asked, "And your Ma?"

Arati looked sad. "She passed away … three years back."

Both of us felt nostalgic. We started to talk about old times. I told her about Soumya and Shreya. About my current activity. She told me about her mother. She also moved to Delhi with Arati. "Ma brought up Apu and Shubho … literally. They also doted on her. Her health was fine … or maybe she never let us know. Passed away in her sleep … not giving us any chance to …" her voice trailed away.

I told her about Dewan's disappointment after she left Calcutta. Her face brightened up at the mention of Dewan and his family. She enquired if we were still in touch. But I was not. We lost touch after I went abroad. She felt disappointed.

Both the trains were announced almost at the same time. So finally it was time for parting again. Arati and Shubho bade goodbye. I was to collect my luggage, so I headed for the cloakroom. Suddenly, I had a distressing feeling that I was going to lose Arati and her son forever again and turned back. I saw that Arati and her son were disappearing in the crowd. I started to run frantically to catch them. I shouted, "Arati…", at the top of my voice. Both of them turned back. There was a pale smile on her face. Was she tormented by the same fear too? I was breathless when I caught them. I fumbled out a business card out of my handbag and also a pen. "Give your contact number…" Arati took the card and looked at it. She opened her vanity bag, kept the card carefully inside, took out a small piece of paper, scribbled a number on it and handed it to me with a faint smile.

I took Shubho in my arms again for a few seconds and then rushed towards the cloakroom.

## THE END